The
GLITTER
Dragon

For Tim with love — C.R.

First North American edition 1995
Published by
Marlowe & Company,
632 Broadway, Seventh Floor,
New York, NY 10012

Copyright © 1995 by
The Templar Company plc

Edited by A.J. Wood
Designed by Janie Louise Hunt

ISBN 1-56924-838-9

Printed and bound in Belgium

The
GLITTER
Dragon

Written by
Caroline Repchuk
Illustrated by
Colin and Moira Maclean

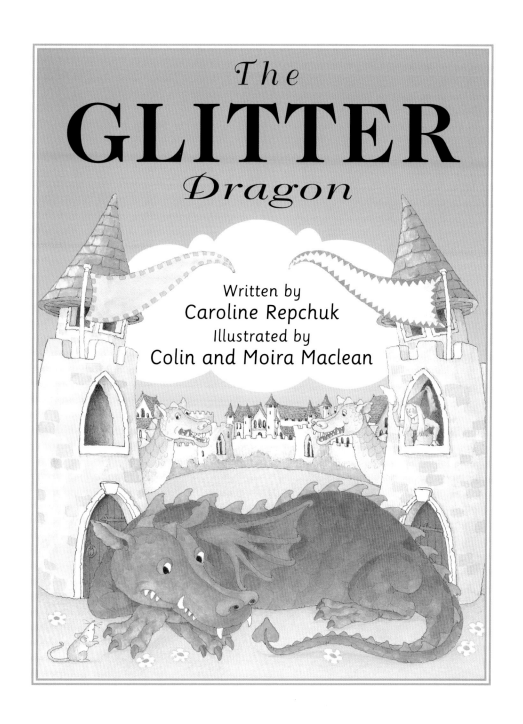

MARLOWE & COMPANY
NEW YORK

HIGH IN A ROCKY HILLSIDE there was once a group of dark and dangerous caves. And living inside them was the most fearful band of dragons you would never hope to meet.

•

The townsfolk that lived in the valley close by trembled at the thought of what lurked and threatened from that hillside. It seemed that Geoffrey was their only hope...

Now, Geoffrey also lived in a cave high in the hillside. And, surprisingly, he was also a dragon. Only Geoffrey wasn't like the other dragons. He wasn't too fond of burning down houses, he said it didn't seem right to leave people without a home. And every time he encountered a maiden, instead of carrying her off to the hills and devouring her for breakfast, he blushed a rather deep shade of crimson and started to stammer.

He said he was awfully
s-s-sorry, but did she have
the t-t-time p-please?

Not at all the way for a proper
dragon to go about things.

But of course the most truly remarkable thing about Geoffrey was his scales. While the other dragons were a dull and dirty bunch, Geoffrey sparkled and shimmered in the light, his scales reflecting a rainbow of colors.

●

Now, you may think that Geoffrey would have been proud of his appearance, but you'd be wrong! In fact he tried everything to disguise his beautiful scales. He even rolled in mud to try and cover them up, which for a nice clean dragon like Geoffrey was quite extreme. But it was no good. The other dragons teased him constantly.

"Call yourself a dragon?" they would sneer. "Why you're nothing but an oversized, overheated, useless tower of tinsel!" Geoffrey hung his head in shame.

So one night he decided to run away. He packed up his pajamas,
his teddy bear and his pink toothbrush in his suitcase,
wrapped himself in a blanket, and set off sadly in search of a new home.

Geoffrey had never been far from home before.
He had never even left the valley. He had no
idea what lay on the other side of the hills,
but he was sure he'd find someone who would
like to share their home with a polite and
friendly dragon like himself.

●

He had not gone far, when he reached the
edge of a dark and dangerous forest.
"Oh dear," quivered Geoffrey, pulling his
blanket around him, "I don't like the dark!"
But he knew it was too late to turn back, so
clutching his teddy bear tightly, he bravely
journeyed on.

Inside the forest Geoffrey had a peculiar feeling that he was being watched. And he was quite right. He was! He stepped nervously forward and WHOOSH! In a whirling, tumbling flash poor Geoffrey found himself dangling upside down from a tree.

"What are you doing in my forest?" boomed a loud voice from below.

•

"M-most awfully sorry to b-bother you," stammered Geoffrey, looking down at a big slimy monster. "It's just that I'm l-looking for a new home."
Just then a shaft of light broke through the trees. Geoffrey's scales glittered in the sun. The monster (who had been looking forward to an early lunch) cried out in alarm. "Ugh, get that horrible shiny light out of my lovely dark forest... NOW!"

Geoffrey landed with a thump
as the monster let go of the rope,
and he scurried out of the forest as fast
as his little legs could carry him, leaving
his blanket and suitcase behind him!

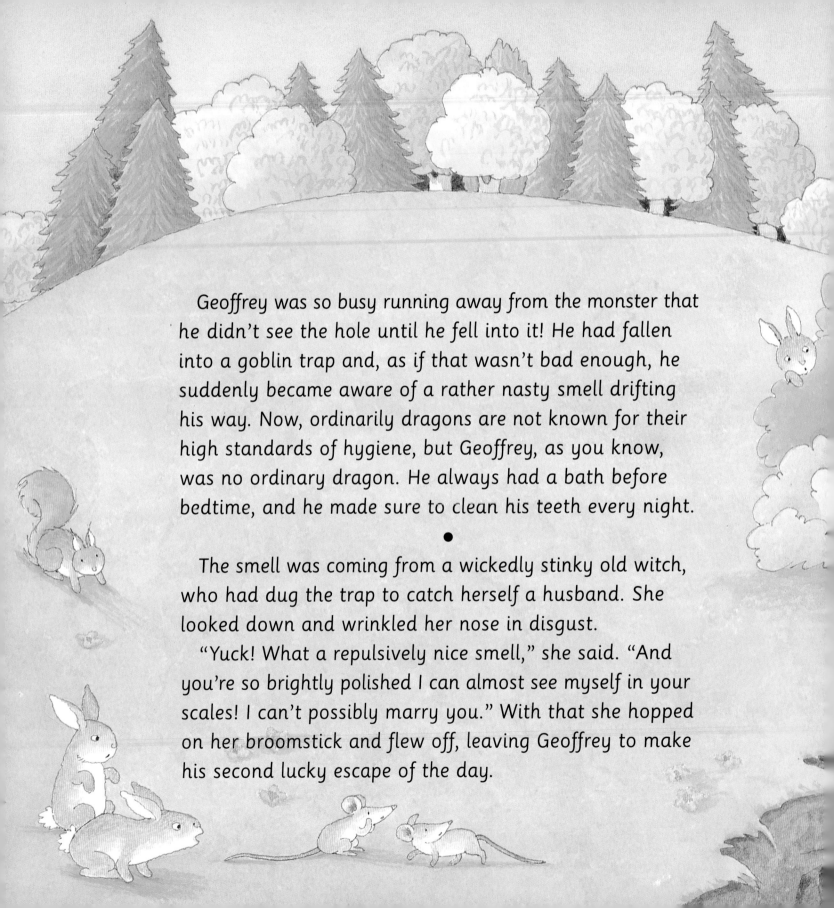

Geoffrey was so busy running away from the monster that he didn't see the hole until he fell into it! He had fallen into a goblin trap and, as if that wasn't bad enough, he suddenly became aware of a rather nasty smell drifting his way. Now, ordinarily dragons are not known for their high standards of hygiene, but Geoffrey, as you know, was no ordinary dragon. He always had a bath before bedtime, and he made sure to clean his teeth every night.

●

The smell was coming from a wickedly stinky old witch, who had dug the trap to catch herself a husband. She looked down and wrinkled her nose in disgust.

"Yuck! What a repulsively nice smell," she said. "And you're so brightly polished I can almost see myself in your scales! I can't possibly marry you." With that she hopped on her broomstick and flew off, leaving Geoffrey to make his second lucky escape of the day.

But Geoffrey had not gone far when he felt the ground quiver. He looked around nervously, but there was nothing to see. Seconds later the earth shook so violently he thought it must be an earthquake. Frantically he looked around for shelter. This time there was something to see. A foot the size of a football field had appeared right next to him. It belonged to an enormous giant.

"Aha! What have we here?" boomed the giant in a voice as loud as a ship's horn. "A nice, shiny beetle for my bug collection!"

•

But, hard as he tried, the giant could not catch Geoffrey. His glittering scales were just too slippery! Geoffrey ran around and around until the spinning giant felt very dizzy and came tumbling to the ground with a huge CRASH! Geoffrey was off in a flash, heading for the mountains. Perhaps he'd find a nice new cave there. Bug collection indeed!

It didn't take long for Geoffrey to find a warm, dry cave in the mountainside. He crawled inside, curled up, and fell fast asleep at once, worn out by his adventures.

He was awakened by the sound of heavy footsteps—lots of heavy footsteps. "And just what do you think you are doing in our cave, tinsel toes?" growled a voice. Cautiously Geoffrey opened one eye, and looked up. In front of him stood the biggest, meanest bunch of dragons he had ever seen. "Um, I'm er, d-dreadfully s-sorry," he stammered. "I think I m-must have made a m-mistake."

"A really big mistake," said the biggest, meanest dragon of all. "So we'll have to teach you a lesson."

Minutes later Geoffrey found himself tied to a cliff face. Foaming sea crashed on the rocks far below him.

All day he was lashed and pounded by the howling wind and salty spray, and as darkness fell and the sky turned inky black, Geoffrey began to wonder if he would live till morning.

Just then he spotted a dark shape looming on the horizon. It was a ship— a very grand ship indeed. Geoffrey began to feel nervous. The ship was heading straight toward the rocks.

"L-look out!" called Geoffrey, but his feeble cry was lost on the wind.

Geoffrey squeezed his eyes tightly shut and waited for the crash. But just then the bright full moon came shimmering into view. And so did Geoffrey!

Broad beams of moonlight reflected from his scales and shone out into the darkness like beacons. Loud cries came from the deck, and Geoffrey watched with relief as the helmsman turned the mighty ship's wheel. Without a second to spare the huge ship swung aside and passed safely around the rocks.

Safely, that is, for all but the Royal Princess Petunia. As the ship swung aside, she was tossed overboard into the foaming, heaving sea. Geoffrey paled in horror as he realized that only he had seen her, and only he could save her! There was not a moment to lose.

Mustering all his strength, Geoffrey gave a mighty tug and broke free from his chains. Then, spreading his magnificent sparkling wings wide, he swooped down and scooped the Princess up from the stormy waters.

High on Geoffrey's glittering back, the Princess returned in triumph to her kingdom. And it just so happened that it was Geoffrey's homeland too! The Princess was so grateful that she threw her arms around him and kissed his cheek with a resounding SMACK! "My hero..." she sighed. Geoffrey blushed a deep shade of crimson. "G-gosh. Th-thank you very much," he managed to stutter.

•

Then something very strange happened.
There was a loud BANG!!! a blinding flash of light, and there in the place of Geoffrey the glitter dragon stood...

...a dashingly handsome knight in shining armor! "C-crikey," he stuttered. "I'm back! You've broken the spell."

Princess Petunia was delighted. Her very own knight in shining armor—what a stroke of luck! "Will you marry me?" she asked boldly. Geoffrey blushed a very deep shade of crimson. "It w-would be my p-pleasure," he stuttered...

●

Geoffrey and Petunia talked long into the night. He told her of how a wicked witch had changed him into a dragon, and that only the kiss of a Princess could save him. He'd tried hard to maintain his dashing good looks, but had found that Princesses weren't generally attracted to dragons, no matter how clean their teeth were. He had given up hope of ever changing back.

And so the Princess and her knight were married,

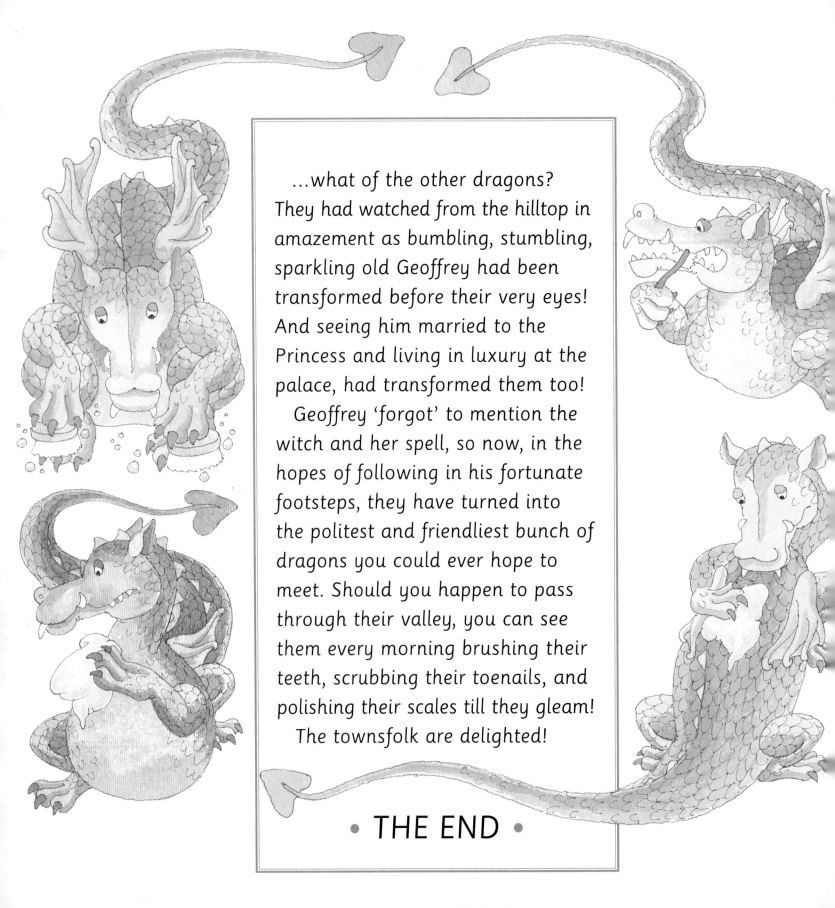

...what of the other dragons? They had watched from the hilltop in amazement as bumbling, stumbling, sparkling old Geoffrey had been transformed before their very eyes! And seeing him married to the Princess and living in luxury at the palace, had transformed them too!

Geoffrey 'forgot' to mention the witch and her spell, so now, in the hopes of following in his fortunate footsteps, they have turned into the politest and friendliest bunch of dragons you could ever hope to meet. Should you happen to pass through their valley, you can see them every morning brushing their teeth, scrubbing their toenails, and polishing their scales till they gleam! The townsfolk are delighted!

• THE END •